L○ST

IN THE SEA OF DESPAIR

TRACEY TURNER

Crabtree Publishing Company
www.crabtreebooks.com

Crabtree Publishing Company
www.crabtreebooks.com
1-800-387-7650

616 Welland Ave.
St. Catharines, ON
L2M 5V6

PMB 59051, 350 Fifth Ave.
59th Floor,
New York, NY

Published by Crabtree Publishing Company in 2015.

Author: Tracey Turner

Illustrator: Nelson Evergreen

Project coordinator: Kelly Spence

Editors: Alex Van Tol, Kathy Middleton

Proofreader: Wendy Scavuzzo

Prepress technician: Ken Wright

Print and Production coordinator:
Katherine Berti

Text copyright © 2014 Tracey Turner

Illustration copyright © 2014 Nelson Evergreen

Copyright © 2014 A & C Black

Additional images © Shutterstock

First published 2014 by A & C Black, an imprint of Bloomsbury Publishing Plc.

The author and publisher accept no responsibilty for any accidents that occur as a result of this book.

WARNING!
The instructions in this book are for extreme survival situations only. Always proceed with caution, and ask an adult to supervise—or, if possible, seek expert help. If in doubt, consult a responsible adult.

Printed in Canada / 102014 / EF20140925

**Library and Archives Canada
Cataloguing in Publication**

Turner, Tracey, author
    Lost in the sea of despair / Tracey Turner.

(Lost : can you survive?)
Includes index.
ISBN 978-0-7787-0731-8 (bound).--
ISBN 978-0-7787-0739-4 (pbk.)

    1. Plot-your-own stories. I. Title.

PZ7.T883Losti 2014   j823'.92
C2014-904026-1

**Library of Congress
Cataloging-in-Publication Data**

Turner, Tracey.
  Lost in the Sea of Despair / by Tracey Turner ;
illustration, Nelson Evergreen. -- American edition.
     pages cm. -- (Lost: can you survive?)
  ISBN 978-0-7787-0731-8 (reinforced library
binding) -- ISBN 978-0-7787-0739-4 (pbk.)
  1. Plot-your-own stories. [1. Survival--Fiction. 2.
Pacific Ocean--Fiction. 3. Sea stories. 4. Plot-
your-own stories.] I. Evergreen, Nelson, 1971-
illustrator. II. Title.

  PZ7.T8585Ls 2014
  [Fic]--dc23

                                    2014033167

Contents

Asia

North Pacific Ocean

Central America

South America

5

Australia

New Guinea

Micronesia

Melanesia

Polynesia

Pitcairn Islands

New Zealand

South Pacific Ocean

Antarctica

Welcome to your adventure!
STOP! Read this first!

Welcome to an action-packed adventure in which you take the starring role!

You're about to become lost at sea in the vast Pacific Ocean, battling against towering waves, raging storms, and deadly sharks. Choose from different options on each page, according to your instincts, knowledge, and intelligence, and navigate your own way to safety.

You decide:

- How to spot a venomous shellfish
- What to do when you're surrounded by hungry hammerhead sharks
- How to find food on a desert island

. . . and how to survive many more life-or-death dilemmas. Along the way, you'll discover the facts you need to help you stay alive.

It's time to test your survival skills—or die trying!

Your adventure starts on page 7.

You watch helplessly as the small orange life raft bobs out of sight in the churning waves. You clutch the railing of the yacht as another massive wave crashes over you, wondering how on Earth you're going to survive.

Tonight's terrible events swirl around in your head like a nightmare. Your uncle woke you up when he discovered the small yacht was letting in water from a hole in the hull, or body of the boat. It was the middle of the night, and a storm was raging around you—so different from when you had set off on this trip, sailing into the South Pacific on a calm, sunny day. Trying to repair the hole, your uncle got washed overboard. He shouted for you to throw him a life raft. You saw him inflate it and climb into it, then the sight of the tiny raft got lost among gigantic waves.

Your uncle is an experienced sailor, but you have no knowledge of sailing at all. Yet here you are, far from land, surrounded by crashing waves in a leaking boat. The yacht rolls up and down the waves, nearly hurling you into the sea. You are lost in the Pacific—and completely alone.

How will you survive?

Turn to page 8 to find information you need to help you survive.

The Pacific Ocean is enormous. It is the largest of the world's oceans, covering roughly 28% of Earth's surface, stretching from the Arctic in the north to the waters of the Antarctic in the south. The Pacific is bounded by Asia and Australia to the west, and North and South America to the east.

You are lost in the tropical South Pacific. The sea here is dotted with islands, and you might be lucky enough to find one—but there is a lot more sea than land. The islands of the South Pacific are some of the most remote in the world, scattered over 12,000 square miles (31,000 sq km). Many people have become lost in the Pacific Ocean, never to be seen again. If you're going to survive, you'll need to have your wits about you.

Perils of the South Pacific

The open sea is probably the most challenging survival environment of all. No one can survive in cold water for very long but, here in the tropics, you stand a much better chance of staying alive. Besides the perils of surviving on a tiny boat in a huge sea, you will have to brave brutal tropical storms, sharks, whales, and other large marine mammals that could capsize your craft. Closer to shore, sea jellies, sea snakes, stingrays, and other venomous sea creatures might be lurking. If you do find land, you need to be aware of fatal diseases such as malaria and be wary of any animals you might meet.

Island Life

There are thousands of islands in the South Pacific. The region is divided geographically into Micronesia, Melanesia, and Polynesia. The largest island is New Guinea, which covers nearly 270,270 square miles (700,000 sq km). The smallest inhabited island is Pitcairn at just two square miles (5 sq km). There are thousands of uninhabited islands, too, some even smaller than Pitcairn. Often, the reason an island is uninhabited is because there's no fresh water available. The islands are dramatically different. There are different cultures, languages, wildlife, and plant life. The farther west you go, the more plants and animals you'll find. Farther east, there are fewer species.

Turn to page 10.

Basic Survival Tips at Sea

Here are a few basic tips that might affect your chances of survival at sea.

- Onboard any boat, always find out where the life rafts, life belts, and life jackets are, and make sure you're familiar with emergency drills.

- Stay with the boat for as long as possible before abandoning it for a life raft. A large boat will have more supplies on board and be easier for rescuers to spot than a smaller raft.

- If you can, let Search and Rescue services know you are abandoning your boat for a life raft.

- If a call for help has been successfully sent, stay in the same position. Life rafts have sea anchors that stop them from drifting. If a call hasn't been sent, keep the raft moving.

- Make sure you're protected from the elements as much as possible.

- Drinking fresh water is a priority. If you don't have a desalinator to remove salt from seawater (see page 23), find ways to collect rain or make a solar still (see page 45). Never drink seawater.

- Take deep breaths and stay calm. Panicking will seriously reduce your chances of survival.

Remember, this book is not intended as an official guide to sailing trips.

Turn to page 11.

The storm is dying down a bit, but the little yacht is still pitching wildly from side to side.

The hole in the side of the hull is still letting in water. Now that you can move around more easily and safely, you open the door to the cabin. Water is everywhere! There's no way the bilge pump can keep up with this. You start bailing the water out over the side with a bucket. You're bailing faster than the water is coming in, but you wonder how long you can keep it up.

There is a second life raft. You spotted it when you picked up the first one, and your uncle shouted to you that you might need to use it. Maybe it would be better to abandon the boat now and set off in the other life raft?

If you decide to abandon ship, go to page 36.

If you decide to stay with the yacht, go to page 20.

By choosing to inflate the life raft on the side of the listing hull, you're going to make life very difficult for yourself. This is the windward side of the yacht, which means the wind is blowing toward you. Not only will you have to jump down into it with the wind blowing in your face, but the life raft risks becoming ripped on the barnacles that cling to the bottom of the boat.

In the first glimmer of dawn light, you throw the raft over the side. You follow the instructions on the outside of the life raft's canister, pulling on a long cord to make it inflate. Just when you're starting to think there must be something wrong with it, the life raft pops open with a loud hissing noise. The raft inflates, its canopy pops up automatically, and you jump down into it over the side of the yacht's hull. Now you have to push the life raft away from the yacht. But, before you have a chance to do this, a wave smashes the raft into the hull.

Your blood freezes as you hear an ominous ripping sound, then air hissing out of the raft. Panic-stricken, you consider trying to get back onto the boat, abandoning the raft. If it's torn, how long can it last? But, luckily for you, there's a second inflation compartment on this life raft, and you hear it inflating automatically. Whew!

Go to page 15.

You take out the paddle and splash it down on the surface of the water. The turtle doesn't seem to notice. You feel another bump underneath the raft—it's another turtle! Looking at the barnacles clinging to the turtles' rough shells, you worry it's only a matter of time before they scrape and tear the bottom of the raft. You bash the paddle right next to the head of one of the turtles. Alarmed, it begins to swim away. The other one follows it.

You're relieved. You're checking underneath the raft, peering down into the blue sea, when the sun slips out from behind a cloud and you're able to see more clearly. But what you see makes the hairs on the back of your neck stand up. Your heart races—underneath the raft are the unmistakable shapes of five large hammerhead sharks.

It worked with the turtles. Maybe you should slap the water with the paddle to drive away the sharks, too.

If you decide to use the paddle to drive away the sharks, go to page 74.

If you decide not to, go to page 30.

After awhile, the raft starts to lurch sickeningly from side to side. You think the sea is getting rougher again, and you zip up the raft's canopy, grimly accepting the idea of another storm on its way.

You were starting to feel sick anyway, and now that you can't see outside the raft, you feel an awful lot worse. You put your hands over your mouth and concentrate hard on not being sick. But it's no good—in a rush, you unzip the canopy, stick your head out, and vomit into the sea.

You lie down, feeling terrible, and take some seasickness pills.

Go to page 32.

The little life raft bobs along on its precarious way. You hope that you'll be rescued or find land before anything else has a chance to tear the raft. You used up your secondary inflation before you even started.

You're unlucky, though. The raft comes supplied with a sharp knife, and you take it out of its sheath to have a look at it. You drop it, point first onto your inflated raft. It pierces the raft.

You scramble for the raft's repair kit. You're panicking, but you manage to stick a patch on and bail out the water that has leaked in. The patch doesn't last very long, though. You can't bail fast enough and, inevitably, the raft starts to take in more and more water until it sinks—taking you down with it.

The end.

The boat has completely overturned now, and you climb up on top of the hull. The sun has come up, and you scan the sky for a helpful plane or helicopter. But there's nothing but heavy, gray clouds in the sky, and you can't see anything on the horizon except white-topped waves.

Go to page 24.

The turtles must be interested in your raft because they keep swimming underneath it, from one side to the other. Maybe they're finding something to eat under there. Whatever the reason, you become increasingly worried about the turtles' hard shells rubbing against the bottom of the raft.

You're right to be worried. The turtles have worn away at the raft's strong fabric. As one of the turtles disappears underneath the raft for what seems like the hundredth time, you hear the bottom of the raft tear. Your heart pounds—the air is hissing out of one section of the life raft's buoyant air compartments! Luckily, though, the life raft has a secondary buoyancy layer, so there's no need to attempt a repair. At least, not for now.

The turtles swim away. You're going to try to frighten them away if they come back—there aren't any more chances if they damage the raft again.

Go to page 38.

Unfortunately, splashing the surface of the sea doesn't alarm the sharks at all. In fact, it makes them more curious—the predators are attracted to splashing that might be a fish thrashing near the surface. This is exactly the kind of thing sharks seek out.

The sharks become so interested that they take a bite out of the paddle to find out what it is. . . then the raft. . . then you.

The end.

Hammerhead Sharks

- The strange shape of the hammerhead's head is thought to help them find their prey more easily. Their eyes are set wide apart, and their heads also contain special organs that sense other creatures. They can see and sense a wide area.

- Hammerheads prey on fish, shellfish, octopus, squid, and their favorite food, stingrays. Their special sensory organs help them find the stingrays even when they're buried under sand. They use their hammer-shaped heads to pin stingrays to the sea floor as they attack.

- There are different species of hammerhead. Most types are quite small and are not usually dangerous to people. The largest, the great hammerhead, can grow up to 20 feet (6 m) long—this is the type you've just encountered.

- Hammerheads are found all over the world, in tropical seas and cooler seas, and they will swim close to land and far out at sea.

The storm has died down even more and you keep bailing out the water coming in through the hole. As the first light of dawn appears, the full horror of your predicament becomes clear—the yacht is obviously sinking. It's only a matter of time before it goes under no matter how quickly you bail, and you're already exhausted. You take a look at the waterlogged radio, flicking the switches on and off, but there's no sign of life.

It looks as though it's time to inflate the life raft. But maybe you'd be better off staying with the yacht? After all, it's much bigger and easier to spot than a little raft.

If you decide to stay with the sinking boat, go to page 16.

If you decide to inflate the life raft, go to page 36.

Abandoning Ship

It's a good idea to stay with a boat or ship until the point of no return. It's easier for rescuers to see a boat than a life raft, and there are more things in it that can help you survive. But once it's clear the boat is sinking, there's nothing else you can do but abandon ship.

- Stay calm! Panic will lead to bad decisions.

- If you can, send distress calls.

- If the shore or other ships are nearby, fire distress flares.

- Put on extra clothes, to keep as warm as you can, and a life jacket.

- Take seasickness pills.

- Find the Emergency Grab Bag (see page 23).

- Prepare to launch the life raft (see page 37).

You throw the life raft over the side of the yacht, which is now listing close to the surface of the sea. The raft comes in a canister, and there are instructions telling you to pull out a long rope to its fullest length, then give it a sharp tug. As you give the final tug, the raft inflates by itself with a loud hiss as gas rushes into the raft's inflatable compartments. You'd be impressed if you weren't so terrified.

Just before you abandon the yacht and jump into the raft, you spot something else that might help. Next to the wheel you spot a large bag labeled Emergency Grab Bag.

Once in in the raft, you investigate the raft and the Grab Bag. Among other things, you notice seasickness pills and sick bags. You feel OK at the moment, but maybe you should take some pills to be on the safe side?

If you decide to take seasickness pills, go to page 32.

If you decide not to go to page 14.

Emergency Grab Bag

There are lots of useful things in the life raft, but the Grab Bag contains some life-saving extras:

- The most important object is a desalinator. Operated by a hand pump, the desalinator makes seawater drinkable if you follow the instructions. You can make about four cups (1 L) of drinkable water an hour—more than enough to allow you to survive. If it weren't for the desalinator, you'd have to make a solar still (see page 45), or collect rainwater or water that's condensed inside the raft.

Other useful items include:

- A small waterproof bag of toiletries, including a toothbrush, toothpaste, sunscreen, and lip balm

- Dry clothing, including a sun hat, sunglasses, and lightweight, thermal blankets in a waterproof bag

- A pack of cards

- Extra seasickness pills and sick bags (there are some already in the life raft)

- Matches in a waterproof container

The sea is getting rougher. You begin to realize that you've been foolish to stay with the yacht instead of inflating the life raft. You can't reach anything that can help you survive. Inside the life raft, you would have had all sorts of useful things. But it's impossible to get to it now.

Things get worse—water must have filled a large space inside the yacht, because one end of it slumps downward. The boat is starting to sink.

After the boat has sunk, you cling to some cushions that have floated to the surface. Eventually they start to sink, too. You soon become exhausted and cold. You drown.

The end.

Open Sea Survival

- You will only be able to survive in cold water for a short time before hypothermia sets in. Depending on the temperature, this could be only a matter of minutes.

- In very cold water, people go into shock right away, breathing uncontrollably fast and deep. This lasts about three minutes. If someone goes under the water during that time, they will swallow water and drown. Otherwise, people can survive for up to about 20 minutes in temperatures as low as 41°F (5°C).

- Water pulls heat from the body much faster than air does. The more of a person's body that is underwater, the faster they will lose heat. If you can find something to float on, you will be better off.

- Even if the water temperature is as high as 80°F (27°C), it can be dangerous. Heat will still be lost from the body. However, people will survive much longer in warmer water before they lose heat and become hypothermic.

- If you find yourself submerged in water and can't climb onto something floating, keep your arms and legs tucked in close to avoid losing heat. This will be difficult unless you have a life jacket.

You slowly and carefully edge toward the bird, hanging on to the outside of the raft. It cocks its head to one side, staring at you with a beady eye, but it doesn't look alarmed. You inch closer. It's almost within your grasp. Just a bit farther and you'll be able to grab the bird's legs . . .

You lunge for the bird, which takes off with a loud squawk of alarm. You slip on the outside of the raft and plunge into the sea. A wave carries you away from the raft. You struggle in the water to get back to it, but the distance between you and the raft becomes greater and greater.

You bitterly regret trying to catch the bird. It's your final thought before you become too tired to continue swimming—and drown.

The end.

Pacific Sea Birds

- Red-footed and brown boobies are the two species of boobies likely to be found in the South Pacific. The bird you tried to catch is a red-footed booby. Blue-footed boobies live in the Galapagos Islands and along the Pacific coasts of North and South America.

- Red-footed boobies live in the Atlantic, Pacific, and Indian Oceans, and often land on boats. They nest on land, but can fly more than 93 miles (150 km) looking for food—usually fish or squid—and can dive as deep as 100 feet (30 m) after prey.

- As well as boobies, noddies are found in the South Pacific, especially brown noddies, which also live in the Caribbean, the Red Sea, and the Indian Ocean, and blue noddies, which nest on islands in the South Pacific.

- You might also spot great frigatebirds, which sometimes chase other birds to get them to drop or regurgitate their fish. Males have a red pouch in their throats that they inflate like a balloon to attract female frigatebirds.

- Watch which way birds fly in the evening. They are heading in the direction of land.

You spend a sleepless night, tossing and turning and wondering what that bump was. Every so often, you feel something else nudge the bottom of the raft. You desperately want to go to sleep and forget about it. Even if you knew what was making the bumps, what could you do about it? Finally, you manage to drift off into a fitful sleep for a few hours.

Go to page 54.

Whales and Dolphins

The South Pacific is home to different species of whales and dolphins, some of which you might meet because they're curious animals. The bumps you felt were made by curious bottlenose dolphins. Here are a few species of whales and dolphins that live in the South Pacific:

- Bottlenose and spinner dolphins are the marine acrobats of the South Pacific, performing amazing leaps and spins (as the spinner dolphin's name suggests). They can reach speeds of up to 18 miles (30 km) per hour. Dolphins of different species sometimes come together to form enormous pods of a thousand or more animals.

- Huge humpback whales can be up to 65 feet (20 m) long and could easily overturn a raft with a flick of their tail. The island of Tonga, in the South Pacific, is a breeding ground for humpback whales.

- Pilot whales are usually found in deeper water in pods of between 10 and 30. William Butler (see page 118) blamed a pod of pilot whales for sinking his yacht in the Pacific.

Every so often, you peer outside of the raft. The menacing, unmistakable shapes are still there. There are more of them than you thought—you count nine. You decide not to look and try to concentrate instead on a game of solitaire with your deck of cards, hoping that the sharks will get bored and go away.

Eventually, after an hour or two of worrying about the hammerheads, you risk another look into the sea. They're gone! They must have caught the scent of something more interesting in the water. (To find out more about hammerhead sharks, go to page 19.)

You're starting to wonder when you'll spot another yacht or a ship or maybe even an island. You unzip the front of the raft and take a good look around. The sun is shining in a clear blue sky—no sign of a plane. Suddenly a dark shape in the water catches your eye. You very much wish it hadn't. It's huge—a 10-foot- (3 m) long creature, just below the surface and a short distance from the raft. As the raft moves, blown by the wind and pushed by currents, the creature moves with it. You can clearly see by its shape that the creature is a huge shark with a rounded, white-tipped dorsal fin, and it's following you.

▶ Go to page 43.

Oceanic Whitetip Sharks

The shark that's following your raft is an oceanic whitetip, considered to be one of the most dangerous sharks to humans.

- Oceanic Whitetips live in warmer waters out in open sea and are rarely seen close to land.

- Whitetips are usually solitary animals, but they sometimes group together in a feeding frenzy if there's an opportunity for a good meal, such as a dead whale.

- These sharks aren't fussy about what they eat—fish, turtles, seabirds, octopuses, crabs, dead whales, and dolphins. They have extremely powerful jaws.

- Whitetips can be aggressive toward other sharks and are also dangerous to people, though they rarely come into contact with people because of where they live.

- During World War II, oceanic whitetips were blamed for the deaths of many soldiers who survived their ships being sunk by torpedoes and bombs in tropical seas.

- Whitetips are curious and show no fear of divers—another reason they're considered highly dangerous.

- Whitetips can measure up to about 13 feet (4 m) long, although most are smaller. There are other much bigger sharks, such as great whites, which can reach up to about 21 feet (6.5 m).

Rain lashes the raft, and the wind howls. Worst of all, huge waves send the raft plummeting down into deep troughs of water, then carry it back up again in a terrible rollercoaster ride. In fact, it's a hundred times worse than the most stomach-turning, theme-park ride you've ever been on.

Every time you feel the raft climbing an impossibly tall wave, you think it's going to overturn and sink on the way down—but it doesn't. The raft always rights itself. You brace yourself, clinging onto the raft's handholds as the storm hurls you around.

Go to page 44.

Pacific Storms

- Storms in which the winds reach speeds of more than 73 miles (118 km) per hour are classified as typhoons.

- Hurricanes, typhoons, and cyclones are all the same type of weather, but different names are used in different areas: in the Atlantic and northeast Pacific, it's a hurricane; in the northwest Pacific, it's a typhoon; and in the South Pacific and Indian Ocean, it's a cyclone.

- These violent storms are caused by warm air rising quickly and getting pushed aside as it cools, causing it to spin.

- Cyclones, hurricanes, and typhoons are identified by names. The first storm of the year is given a name beginning with the letter A, the next beginning with B, and so on. If a storm does a lot of damage, that name is never used again.

- The tropical cyclone season in the South Pacific runs from November to April.

With the storm finally over, the sea calms down, until the raft is rocking gently on the waves. It's an enormous relief not to feel yourself being hurled around the ocean, and gradually you stop feeling sick.

You're drifting, enjoying the peace and comfort, when something bumps the bottom of the raft. Quickly, you unzip the canopy and look out. You can't see anything. Maybe it was a piece of driftwood. You feel another bump, quite strong this time. Watery sunlight is making its way through the gray clouds. You can make out a round shape emerging from underneath the raft. It's a turtle! The creature surfaces.

It's quite big—almost three feet (1 m) long, you reckon— with a reddish-brown shell covered in barnacles. Uh oh. That means it could rip the life raft if it carries on bumping you from underneath. Maybe you should try to frighten it away.

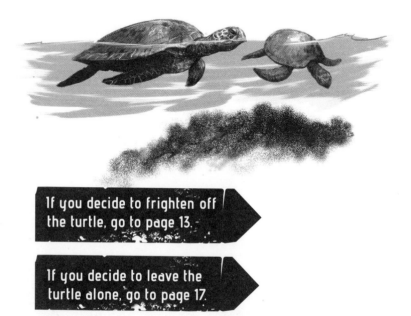

If you decide to frighten off the turtle, go to page 13.

If you decide to leave the turtle alone, go to page 17.

Sea Turtles

- Several different types of turtles live in the Pacific Ocean: green sea, Pacific black sea, hawksbill, leatherback, and loggerhead.

- Green sea turtles, which you've just encountered, are the largest hard-shelled turtles. Their shells can reach five feet (1.5 m) in diameter. The turtles are named for the color of their skin, not their shell. Loggerhead turtles' shells measure up to about 3 feet (1m).

- The largest turtles of all are leatherbacks. They have soft shells that can measure six feet (2 m) long. The largest one ever recorded measured 8.5 feet (2.6 m) long and weighed over 1,984 pounds (900 kg).

- Turtles hatch from eggs on sandy beaches, then travel hundreds of miles out to sea. Female turtles often return to lay their own eggs on the beach where they were hatched.

- Turtles are carnivores. They eat sea jellies (which they sometimes confuse with plastic bags), crabs and other shellfish, and fish. Occasionally, they eat seaweed, too.

- Turtles are often featured in the myths and legends of Pacific Island people. They used to be a sacred food that only noble people were allowed to eat.

You pull the life raft canister off the wall and try to make sense of it. You force yourself to breathe slowly and stop panicking—you know that you won't be able to figure it out if you don't calm down. Taking deep breaths, you read the instructions. It says the raft inflates automatically. Apparently you have to throw the canister into the sea, still hanging on to a rope sticking out of one side. Then you pull the rope to inflate it. You're worried that it's not going to work.

The hole in the yacht has let in more water while you've been trying to figure out the life raft's instructions. The yacht is now listing over to one side. Where should you launch the life raft? On the side that is closest to the water? Or should you throw the raft over the other side of the boat, next to the part of hull that's out of the water?

If you decide to launch the raft on the side nearest to the water, go to page 22.

If you decide to launch it on the other side, near the yacht's hull, go to page 12.

Life Rafts

There are different types of life rafts. Some come in hard canisters and inflate automatically. Thankfully you have one of these, and it's a good one.

- The raft has a canopy arch for high-visibility. It covers the whole raft and inflates automatically. It has a door that zips open and closed.

- There are two buoyancy compartments. If one gets a hole in it, the other one keeps the raft afloat.

- The life raft comes equipped with various items to help you survive: a bailer, paddles, a knife, a mirror for signaling, a flashlight, a horn and a whistle for making noise that's more likely to be heard than shouting, a compass, a first-aid kit, sponges, flares, seasickness pills and sick bags, a pump to top up the inflatable compartments of the raft, a fishing line and hook, and a repair kit.

- The raft should be able to keep you alive for at least 30 days.

You try to make yourself comfortable. Who knows how long it will be before you're rescued?

You arrange the waterproof bag of clothes as a pillow and spread out the blankets underneath you. You're feeling much calmer now. You're also feeling hungry. There's one obvious source of food, and you're completely surrounded by it. Should you try your hand at fishing? You think you saw a fishing line in the life raft pack.

If you decide to fish, go to page 46.

If you decide not to, go to page 42.

Fishing

- The tropical waters of the South Pacific are teeming with life. Fish that you catch in the open sea should be safe to eat. However, any fish you catch that live in shallower waters close to land could be poisonous, so be careful.

- Most fish that have just been caught are safe to eat raw.

- You might even find that flying fish leap into your life raft without you having to catch them!

- When you're fishing, don't handle the fishing line with bare hands because it can be very sharp, especially when sea salt sticks to it. A fishing line could also damage the life raft.

- You'll have to do the messy job of gutting any fish you catch. Cut any fish you don't eat right away into thin strips and hang them up to dry. That way, they may stay safe to eat for a day or two. Any fish you don't gut immediately will go bad quickly.

- You could also catch and eat turtles, though this could be gruesome and difficult, and you risk damaging the raft.

You gather up some dry grass for tinder. Then you make piles out of twigs and some larger pieces of driftwood. There's a breeze blowing, so you dig a hole and line it with stones for a fire pit. Soon you have a cheerful fire burning. There's no shortage of fuel for making fires here (see page 41). You'll be warm and dry, and able to cook food.

At the thought of food, your stomach rumbles. You could go to the seashore and fish. On the other hand, you think you might have spotted a much easier source of protein—there are lots of fat crickets hopping around at the edge of the forest. You know that people eat insects in many different parts of the world. They're all around you and are easy to catch.

If you decide to go fishing, go to page 80.

If you decide to catch some insects, go to page 90.

Making a Fire

- Before you start, gather together everything you'll need: matches, tinder (dry, flammable material such as grass), kindling (dry twigs and small branches), and fuel (larger branches).

- Choose a dry, sheltered spot to make your fire.

- Light your tinder. Good tinder will only need a spark to light it.

- Place your kindling in a pyramid around the tinder.

- Gradually add larger pieces of wood. Take care not to add anything too big or too wet in the early stages of the fire or you'll put it out.

- If there are stones available, you could use them to surround the fire or even to line your fire pit. The stones will heat up and give off heat even after the fire has gone out. They'll also stop the fire from spreading out of control. But be careful not to use wet stones, especially ones that have been submerged in water—they can explode!

You're not hungry enough to try fishing just yet. Anyway, you worry that you might pierce the raft if you tried fishing with a hook.

But you do wonder what fish might be lurking down there, if any. You take a look over the side and instantly wish you hadn't. Circling underneath your raft are a group of hammerhead sharks.

Go to page 30.

After awhile of not daring to look, you peer over the side. The menacing dark shape is still there. You know that there is absolutely nothing you can do against an animal of this size and power: if it decides that your raft is prey, you'll just have to hope it's all over quickly.

A few hours later, the sun is beginning to sink beneath the horizon. You've heard sharks are more likely to feed at dusk and dawn. You gulp, take a deep breath, and have another look for the shark. You can't see it! You make another careful check—it's definitely gone! You almost cry with relief.

Something bashes against the top of the raft. What could it be? You're almost too frightened to look but, when you do, you discover a friendly looking seabird with red webbed feet sitting on the top of your raft having a rest.

It occurs to you that you could probably grab the bird quite easily and wring its neck. You need to eat to stay strong—if you allow yourself to become weak, your chances of survival are not good.

If you decide to catch the bird, go to page 26.

If you decide not to, go to page 48.

The storm dies down. The rain has stopped hammering on the raft's canopy, and you're not being thrown around nearly as much, although the waves are still big.

You're thirsty, and you look in the Emergency Grab Bag for something to drink. There's a bottle of water, and you take a grateful swig. There's also a desalinator—a machine that removes salt from seawater to make it drinkable.

You follow the instructions on the desalinator, and use its hand pump to pump seawater through a special filter, which removes almost all the salt. It's quite hard work, and you make a mental note not to use it when it's very hot out. The effort will only make you sweat and lose more water. You're relieved the desalinator was inside the Grab Bag—you won't have to worry about finding enough fresh water to survive.

Go to page 34.

Finding Water at Sea

You need water to live. Without it, you'll die in a few days. Luckily, you have your desalinator to provide drinkable water. If you didn't have it onboard your raft, there are other ways of obtaining drinkable water:

- Collect rainwater in containers. Some life rafts collect rainwater and funnel it into a pouch on the inside of the raft's canopy. Drink rainwater first, because any water you have in bottles will stay drinkable for longer periods.

- Inflatable solar stills are sometimes included with life rafts. You can also make your own solar still. A still is a device that evaporates seawater, then collects water that forms as pure water droplets, or condensation. You fill the bottom of the still with seawater and attach it to the side of the raft. The salt water evaporates in the sun and drinkable water condenses on the inside and runs into a bottle. Solar stills are not very useful in rough seas, because the salt water sloshes around and gets into the condensed water.

- Whatever you do, don't drink seawater. You might die more quickly than if you drink nothing at all. During World War II, some of the survivors from the USS *Indianapolis* drank seawater, began to hallucinate, and drowned as a result.

You use the hook and line in your survival pack, casting the hook away from the raft. You sit and wait. Nothing happens—but maybe it's not surprising since you don't have any bait. You haul in the line so that you can attach something to the hook that might prove interesting to fish.

But disaster strikes. The hook has embedded itself in the bottom of the raft. As you pull in the line, it rips a jagged hole—right where the turtle ripped the raft earlier.

Before you've had a chance to do anything, the raft begins to sink. It's not long before you become exhausted in the water and drown.

The end.

The ship looks like it's too far away to spot a flare. It's better to wait for a closer ship or a plane that has more of a chance of seeing you. That is, if you ever see another ship, you think dejectedly.

Over the next couple of weeks living on the island, you don't see any other sign of human life whatsoever.

Go to page 95.

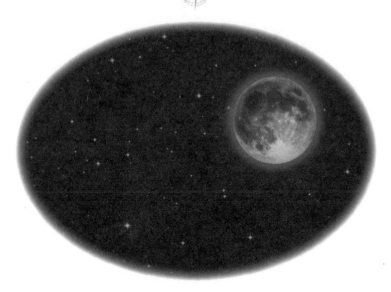

You prepare for your first night aboard the raft. It doesn't seem possible that just 24 hours ago everything was fine—you were on board a sturdy yacht with an experienced sailor and fully functioning radio equipment.

Another bird comes to land on your raft, making you jump. You're glad it's nothing to be frightened of and try to make yourself as comfortable as you can as darkness falls.

Go to page 58.

Signs of Land

There are lots of different signs that land might be nearby. Watch out for these clues:

- Cumulus clouds—the fluffy, cotton candy kind—are often found hovering over or near an island. If the cloud has a flat bottom, that's an even better sign that land is close by.

- More birds are found near land than in the middle of the sea. Notice which way birds fly at dusk. They might be flying toward land to roost. At dawn, they will probably be flying away from the direction of land.

- Lighter colored water means that it's shallower, which could indicate that land is near.

- Look for a greenish tinge in the sky in tropical seas. It might mean that sunlight is being reflected from a shallow lagoon.

- Sniff the air—you might smell muddy swamps.

- Listen for the roar of surf on a beach.

Sure enough, you can feel there's an animal inside the shell. It should make a tasty meal. But, as you tap the shell to try to remove the animal, an agonizing pain shoots up your arm.

You've been bitten by a cone snail. It's quite a large one, and its venom is highly toxic. You're in extreme pain, and your hand and arm swell up. You feel sick, and your muscles become paralyzed. Eventually, you stop breathing and die.

The end.

Cone Snails

- Cone snails are sea snails, and there are different types. The larger ones—which can grow up to about eight inches (20 cm) long—can be extremely venomous. The smaller species have stings that aren't dangerous to people.

- Cone snails inject venom through a sharp, harpoon-like tooth that's strong enough to pierce the shells of other shellfish.

- Cone snails live throughout tropical waters. They live on worms, shellfish, and small fish. The species that live on fish are the most dangerous. Strong, fast-acting poison helps them stop fish from swimming away.

- Cone snails are often brightly colored and patterned. But don't be tempted to pick one up unless you're sure the shell is empty.

- It's extremely rare for people to be bitten and die from a cone snail bite, but it has happened.

You sweep a stick in front of you to check for creepy-crawlies on the forest floor but, in fact, you don't need to worry too much. There are very few small creatures here that can hurt you—at least not seriously.

The island becomes quite steep as you move toward the middle, and it's tough going in the heat. At least you're shielded from the hot sun by the canopy of trees above you.

You suddenly get the feeling you're being watched. You hear a sound and freeze, looking around you warily. Goosebumps prickle on your skin as you listen. There it is again! You swallow hard. Maybe there's someone there. You call "hello." Your voice sound small and shaky, but loud enough for whatever is there to hear you. There's no reply. The sound seemed to come from your left, through some dense foliage. Maybe you should go and investigate.

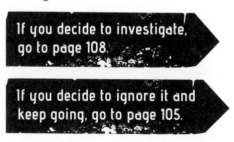

If you decide to investigate, go to page 108.

If you decide to ignore it and keep going, go to page 105.

You lean out of the raft and aim the flare well away from it, making sure your back is to the wind so any sparks from the flare won't touch the raft and sink it. You take off the flare's cover and fire. The flare goes whizzing up into the hazy dawn sky, burning bright red. It burns for about a minute. Surely the ship must see it.

You wait expectantly for the ship to slow down and change course. But nothing happens. The ship doesn't change speed or direction. It sails away from you quickly through the sea. You watch it go until it's just a speck on the horizon.

Many of the large ships that sail the open seas don't have lookouts. Everyone on board was probably asleep.

Go to page 113.

You're woken up by the dawn light and open the zipper on your raft to look out. Who knows what you'll find—maybe a desert island, or a cruise ship, or a pod of friendly dolphins who'll guide you to shore.

Sadly, there's nothing like that. But there is a rain of small splashes on the calm sea in the distance. They come closer as you watch—flying fish, skipping across the ocean toward you.

Soon you spot something else. It looks like a large metal box, and you're heading straight for it. It's a shipping container, floating, at the moment, although it'll eventually sink. Should you let the raft blow toward the container to see what's inside? It might be something useful. Or should you paddle away from it, in case the container harms the raft somehow.

If you decide to paddle away from the container, go to page 88.

If you decide to investigate the container, go to page 92.

Flying Fish

- Flying fish are common in warm seas all over the world. There are about 40 different types, with the largest measuring up to about 18 inches (45 cm) long.

- Flying fish gather enough speed underwater to move about about 37 miles (60 km) per hour. They leap out of the water and spread their fins, which act like wings carrying them through the air.

- Flying fish can sail more than three feet (1 m) above the surface of the water and can cover 650 feet (200 m) in one glide.

- Flying fish are attracted to light, and fishermen use a light at night to catch them. Even when no one's trying to catch them, flying fish sometimes land inside boats!

The raft is encrusted with sea salt. You collect a small handful and eat some. Soon you start to feel better. If you hadn't done this, it might have led to hyponatremia where your body is unable to process water, making the cells in your body expand.

The wind has dropped almost completely. For the first time, the raft isn't pitching and rolling on choppy waves. You drift along slowly in the current.

Go to page 104.

Hyponatremia

- Without enough salt, people can develop hyponatremia, which is a low level of salt in the blood.

- If you drink a lot of water but you don't eat any salt to replace the salt your body loses from sweating, vomiting, or having diarrhea, you could be at risk of hyponatremia. It can also be caused by major organ failure.

- The body's cells swell up with water if there isn't enough salt. It's especially dangerous when brain cells swell. The skull limits how much the brain can expand, causing it to press on the skull.

- Symptoms of hyponatremia include headache, confusion, tiredness, nausea, muscle spasms, and seizures.

- In severe cases, hyponatremia can be fatal.

You're jolted awake. It's the middle of the night, and you can't see a thing. What woke you?

There it is again! A bump underneath the raft. Should you try and find out what's causing it? Or go back to sleep and forget about it?

If you decide to investigate, go to page 78.

If you decide to go back to sleep, go to page 28.

Sailing at Night

- Solo sailors have to sleep but, unlike you, they have radar and sensors to alert them if they're likely to crash into something in the dark.

- Even with electronic equipment, sailors have to keep watch during the night if they're sailing in a shipping lane or if they're close to land.

- Ships have navigation lights so that other ships can see which way they're heading—and whether they're on a collision course!

- On a clear night far from land, you will see many more stars than you can see anywhere else, except in the most remote places on land. In the past, sailors used stars to navigate.

- You might be lucky and see phosphorescence in the sea. Some marine animals and plants glow naturally at night.

The snakes are indeed venomous, and you were right to get away from them even though you would have to try quite hard to get them to bite you. (See page 69 for more information.)

You spot several fish that look as though they'd make a good meal. But you know that there are some poisonous fish that live in tropical reefs and lagoons. Which of these fish should you spear and eat?

If you spear fish A, go to page 66.

If you spear fish B, go to page 75.

You haven't chosen well. The pool is a haven for mosquitoes, which are attracted to the smell of your blood in the night. They feast hungrily on you while you're asleep.

Go to page 84.

You reckon that if you eat just one of the red, pea-like seeds, you'll be OK even if the plant is poisonous. If you get an upset stomach in a few hours, you'll know not to eat anymore of the seeds. You take a seed, crunch it between your teeth, and swallow it.

Unfortunately for you, this plant is very poisonous. Even one seed is enough to kill you if the seed's protective coating is broken. After a few hours, you start vomiting and have diarrhea . . . and it gets worse from there. You are badly dehydrated, too. You drink from your water container, but it's not enough to save you. After a couple of days, your major organs stop working, and you die.

The end.

Rosary Peas

- The rosary pea (scientific name *Abrus precatorius*) is a type of vine native to Africa, Asia, Australia, and parts of the South Pacific. It's known as the rosary pea and also the jewelry plant, because the brightly colored seeds are sometimes used as beads in jewelry or religious necklaces callled rosaries. This isn't recommended though, because of the poison the seeds contain.

- The plant's flowers are small and white, pale pink, or lavender. After flowering, the plant forms seed pods that split open, revealing the brightly colored seeds inside. They are usually bright red with a black cap.

- The seeds contain the toxin abrin. The rosary pea is one of the most poisonous plants in the world.

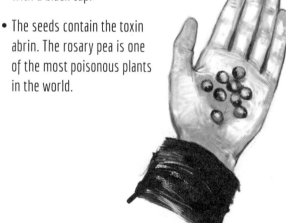

Behind the beach, the forest rises up in a gentle slope that becomes steeper. Maybe you should search in the forest where there are lots of trees and low-growing plants to choose from. On the other hand, it's dark in there, and there might be snakes, spiders, or other creepy-crawlies lurking on the forest floor.

If you decide to search for fruit trees along the beach, go to page 101.

If you decide to look inland, go to page 112.

South Pacific Fruits

- Breadfruit is part of the staple diet of the South Pacific. It's a good source of starch and tastes similar to bread or potatoes when it's cooked. It grows on large evergreen trees and looks like a bumpy melon. You might not have seen it back at home because it doesn't keep well, so it's not exported very often.

- Coconut palms are common. The liquid inside a coconut is sterile, or free from bacteria, as well as tasty. It can even be used in surgical procedures.

- Bananas were likely first grown as a crop in the South Pacific, on the island of New Guinea, around 10,000 years ago. Today, there are hundreds of different varieties. Bunches of bananas don't hang down, as you might think. They point upward.

- Other tropical fruits you might find includes guavas, papayas, and passionfruit.

You manage to spear the fish and triumphantly take it back to the beach. You feed the embers of your fire, roast the fish on a stick, and dig in.

You caught the fish completely by surprise, spearing it before it had even caught sight of you. If it had felt threatened, it might have puffed itself up into a ball, so that the spines on its skin stuck out—which might have made you realize that this is a poisonous pufferfish.

As you're eating the fish, you notice a tingling sensation on your lips and tongue. The poison works quickly—you feel dizzy, weak, and sick. Within minutes, you're lying paralyzed on the sand. A few minutes later, you're dead.

The end.

Pufferfish

- There are lots of different kinds of pufferfish (also known as blowfish), and not all of them are poisonous. But some pufferfish are among the most poisonous animals in the world.

- Some pufferfish only grow to about one inch (2.5 cm) long. The largest species, which lives in fresh water, can measure up to about two feet (60 cm).

- The fish have elastic stomachs that allow them to blow up into a ball several times their usual size.

- The deadly poison contained in pufferfish is tetrodotoxin, which works on the nervous system. There's enough poison in a pufferfish to kill 30 adult humans.

- In Japan, pufferfish is an expensive delicacy, prepared by specially trained chefs who know how to remove the poisonous parts of the fish.

- Some pufferfish are camouflaged, while others are brightly colored to show other animals they're poisonous.

- Pufferfish prey on small shellfish and fish. The larger species of pufferfish can crack open hard shells with their tough beaks.

You are sure you spotted a fish disappearing into these rocks. You feel around inside the rock crevices, and feel a sharp nip. You whip your hand away. Suddenly you feel something on your foot—one of the black-and-white snakes is sinking its fangs into you!

You were right to think that sea snakes aren't usually dangerous. The snakes are indeed venomous—very venomous, in fact—but they rarely bite because they are shy animals. They also have short fangs that don't inject very much venom. Unfortunately, you have threatened them by poking your hands into the rocks where they were hiding, and you have been bitten twice.

You get back to shore before the venom starts to act, but once it does, it's lethal.

The end.

Banded Sea Kraits

- Banded sea kraits live throughout the tropical waters of the South Pacific and Asia, particularly around islands. They can measure up to five feet (1.5 m) long.

- Their venom is 10 times more powerful than a rattlesnake's, but they rarely bite humans and don't inject much venom when they do. When people are bitten, it's usually because sea kraits have become entangled in fishing nets.

- The banded sea krait's powerful venom is used to catch fish and eels. The krait isn't as fast a swimmer as its prey, so it needs a fast-acting venom to stop it's prey from escaping.

- The snakes can stay underwater for up to two hours, but need to surface to breathe air. The banded sea krait is unique among sea snakes because it spends some of its time on land, where it goes to mate, lay eggs, and digest food.

You're in luck—the beach is sandy, and it's easy to jump out into shallow water and drag your raft up onto the sand behind you. Dry land! If you weren't completely exhausted, you'd do a little dance to celebrate.

You haul the raft farther up the beach and decide to make a camp and investigate in the morning. You find the waterproof bag with dry clothes and blankets, change your wet clothes for dry ones, wrap yourself in the blanket, and fall asleep.

The sound of birds wakes you at dawn. The beach is made of fine, silvery-colored sand. You're in a small cove, surrounded by rocks. You decide that the first thing to do is make a shelter. You find a large shallow pool by the rocks on one side of the beach. Maybe that would be a good place for your shelter. Or maybe you should build your shelter near the trees at the edge of the beach.

If you decide to build your shelter near the pool, go to page 61.

If you decide to build it at the forest edge, go to page 89.

Building a Shelter

- The site of your shelter is extremely important. It needs to be on flat ground, away from animal trails, not exposed to the weather, not somewhere that's likely to flood, or where biting insects live.

- Unless you have a desalinator, you'll need to find a source of drinking water. It makes sense to build your shelter near to your water source.

- Caves make good long-term shelters. They are ready-made, and all you need to do is build a covering for the entrance. But check the cave first to make sure it isn't already inhabited by a wild animal. Also check for the possibility of loose rocks that may fall. Unfortunately, there aren't any caves on your beach.

- In a tropical climate, try to raise your shelter off the ground, away from ants, centipedes, spiders, and scorpions.

- If you're feeling up to it, and if there are plenty of fallen logs around, you could try building a log structure. Lay your first layer of logs in a square or rectangle, then cut grooves into the tops of the logs for the next layer to fit into. Make a roof from broad, waxy leaves.

You were right not to eat the plant, in fact, it was a rosary pea, which is very poisonous—just one seed could kill you (see page 63). You do need to eat some fresh fruit or vegetables, though. So you keep on looking.

Go to page 102.

You remove the cap and fire the flare, which makes a spectacular blazing arc high into the sky. Just in case, you take the other one and fire that off, too. Now the ship is bound to see you.

You wait expectantly. The ship continues on its way, showing no sign that it has seen you. You gaze out at the ship as it sails past. How could no one have seen your flare? But the ship is quite a long way away now, and someone would have to have been looking in the right direction to have seen the flares. You've been unlucky.

Muttering curses, you throw the flare case onto the sand. Unfortunately, you don't have any flares left for when you see another ship.

Go to page 100.

You take the paddle and make a big splash in the sea, then turn it over so you're holding the paddle end. You stab downward into the water with the handle. You're hoping the sharks will see this as a threat and swim away.

It doesn't seem to be working, though. If anything, the sharks look as though they're circling closer to the raft.

Go to page 18.

You manage to spear the fish and triumphantly take it back to the beach. You feed the embers of your fire, roast the fish on a stick, and dig in.

You've caught a jackfish, and it tastes delicious. It's just as well you didn't catch the other kind (see page 67). Your jackfish was fine, but sometimes eating certain kinds of larger fish caught on reefs, such as barracudas, groupers, and snappers, can give you ciguatera poisoning. Symptoms include stomach pain, vomiting, and diarrhea. It can last for weeks, although most people recover over time. The fish aren't usually poisonous, but they can carry the poisoning from eating contaminated seaweed. You might be better off sticking to a vegetarian diet from now on.

Go to page 96.

You rub your eyes, because you can hardly believe what you're seeing. You squint into the distance again—it's a ship! And it's coming your way! You're going to be rescued!

But first you have to make sure the ship sees you. Although your raft is bright orange, it's small. You need to do something to make yourself more visible.

In your survival pack, you find some distress flares. One of those should do the trick. On the other hand, the burning flare could damage your raft and sink it. You could signal with the mirror, honk the horn, and blow the whistle. The ship is on course to pass quite close to you. What should you do?

If you decide to use a distress flare, go to page 53.

If you decide to shout and wave, go to page 99.

Shipping Lanes

Shipping lanes are established routes for commercial ships that crisscross the seas around the world.

- The Dover Strait, in the English Channel between England and France, is the world's busiest shipping lane. Around 500 ships per day pass along the route, which makes it hazardous for smaller boats . . . and swimmers trying to cross the channel.

- Another extremely busy shipping lane runs along the Malacca Straits, between the island of Sumatra and Malaysia and southern Thailand, connecting the Indian Ocean with the South China Sea. Shipping in the Malacca Straits is sometimes targeted by pirates. There are around 20 cases of piracy a year.

- Shipping lanes aren't nearly as busy in the South Pacific, but commercial ships do sail along trade routes bound for international destinations, including remote Pacific islands.

You unzip the raft and look out. The sea is fairly calm, the sky is scattered with millions of stars, and there's a bright moon, almost full. You scan the sea for signs of life, desperately hoping you don't see a dorsal fin cutting through the sea toward you. You can't see anything. In fact, the bumps were made by bottlenose dolphins, but they swam away.

As you look across the calm sea, you see the best sight you could possibly have imagined—land! It must be an island—maybe even an inhabited one. You're quite close—close enough to paddle to it—and in the moonlight you can make out a narrow strip of silvery sand. You grab the paddle and get moving.

Go to page 70.

Pacific Islands

- South Pacific islands are scattered across tens of thousands of miles. People first colonized these islands many thousands of years ago. (See page 116 for more on the first Pacific Islanders.)

- The many islands of the South Pacific are divided into the regions of Micronesia, Melanesia, and Polynesia. Cultures and landscapes within those geographic areas can differ widely. Find out about the largest and smallest South Pacific islands on page 9.

- There are lots of other island groups in the Pacific Ocean. The Galapagos Islands, hundreds of miles off the coast of South America in the Pacific, are home to some of the world's most unique animal species. The Philippines, as well as the islands of Indonesia, Taiwan, other Chinese islands, and the islands of Japan, are all in the Pacific. Much farther north, the Aleutian Islands separate the Pacific from the Bering Sea. Most islands in this small chain are part of Alaska.

You do have to take care in this part of the world. There are lots of different dangerous sea creatures lurking where you least expect to find them. Added to that worry, some of the fish that live on reefs and in lagoons are poisonous—even fish that aren't usually poisonous, depending on what they've been eating in the reef (see page 75).

You've been very unlucky because, among the rocks and sand just next to the shoreline, lies a perfectly camouflaged stonefish. A terrible pain shoots into your foot as spines on the stonefish's back pierce it. The stonefish's venom is extremely powerful, and your foot swells very quickly. You collapse on the sand in agonizing pain, unable to move. Within a couple of hours, you're dead.

The end.

Stonefish

- Stonefish are the world's most venomous fish. They live in the shallow waters and coral reefs along tropical coasts.

- Their lumpy, stone-colored bodies look almost exactly the same as the rocks they live among.

- Stonefish venom is carried in the fish's spines along its back, which it raises when threatened.

- The venom is strong and works quickly, but you have a good chance of survival if only some of the spines have penetrated your foot or if the spines haven't pierced your foot too deeply.

- Stonefish can live out of water for up to 12 hours. People have stepped on them while walking along the beach at low tide, away from the sea.

- Stonefish are also known as goblinfish and warty ghouls.

You have to be a pretty good climber to make it up a coconut tree. There aren't any helpful branches to use as footholds. You remember seeing a TV show in which people used a strong scarf to help them climb coconut palms. You take off your T-shirt and use that to help you. Your deck shoes slip, and it takes forever to get even a little way up. But eventually, you get the hang of it.

Unfortunately, you are 20 feet (6 m) off the ground when your T-shirt tears on the bark of the tree. You plummet to the ground, bashing your head on a rock.

The end.

You sharpen a stick to use as a spear, then you swim out to the rocks. The water is calm and clear, and you can see little fish darting all around you. You take a deep breath and dive under the water. There are lots of brightly colored fish here, most of them too small to bother with. But you spot some bigger fish swimming in and around the rocks.

As you get closer to the rocks, your breath almost running out, a white-and-black striped sea snake flashes past you. There's another one disappearing into the rocks. You surface to take a breath.

You are pretty sure that sea snakes aren't dangerous. Should you ignore them and carry on hunting for fish in the rocks?

If you decide to hunt in the rocks, go to page 68.

If you decide to swim away from the sea snakes, go to page 60.

It really wasn't a very good idea to build your shelter right next to this pool. Some of these mosquitoes carry malaria, and you've been bitten by one.

You feel fine for about 10 days, surviving on the island quite happily and feeling confident of rescue. But then you start to feel sick. You have a pounding headache, a high fever, and flu-like symptoms. After a few more days, you start to vomit and have diarrhea. The flu-like symptoms continue.

It takes a while, but the parasites that cause malaria have set up house inside you. Your body does its best to fight them but, with no medical help, you die.

The end.

Malaria

- Only female anopheles mosquitoes can carry malaria. The disease is caused by the plasmodium parasite, a bug that gets into the human bloodstream through the mosquito's bite. There are four types of plasmodium parasites, but only one of them causes malignant, or deadly, malaria. There's another type of malaria that isn't deadly.

- Symptoms usually appear from 10 days to four weeks after you've been bitten, but sometimes people don't get any symptoms for up to a year.

- As long as you are diagnosed with malaria early enough, and you take medicine, malaria probably won't kill you.

- If you come from a country that doesn't have malaria-carrying mosquitoes, you're more at risk because you won't have built up an immunity to the disease.

- Over a million people die from malaria every year, mostly in Africa, because they aren't treated in time.

- Mosquitoes carry other deadly diseases, too, such as yellow fever and dengue fever, both of which can be fatal.

You use the paddle to move the raft closer to one of the floating things. As you dip your hand into the water, you feel a terrible pain—you've been badly stung! You cry out in pain, drop the creature back into the water, and grab your arm.

You've been stung by a Portuguese man-of-war, which looks a a bit like a sea jelly but isn't. They have a sting like a sea jelly, though, and it's extremely painful. You writhe in agony wondering if the sting is fatal. It starts to feel a bit better, and you wash the sting in salt water, keeping well away from the rest of the creatures. The sting has left bright-red marks on your arm.

You doze for the rest of the day, on and off. The wind picks up, and the animals are blown away. After a long snooze, you wake up to find it's nighttime. You take a look out of the raft and immediately forget about the pain in your throbbing arm—there's an island! You start paddling for it.

Go to page 70.

Portuguese Man-of-Wars

- Portuguese man-of-wars, also known as bluebottles, aren't sea jellies. They are floating colonies of closely-related creatures that can't survive alone. The animal floats on its bluish-colored, gas-filled bladder, trailing venomous tentacles deep into the water. The tentacles can reach as long as 164 feet (50 m).

- They get their name from an 18th-century Portuguese sailing ship called a man-of-war. The floating bladders look a bit like the ship's sail (if you squint a bit).

- Portuguese man-of-wars are carnivores and use their tentacles to catch their prey (usually fish).

- They can't move on their own, but are blown along by the wind or moved on ocean currents.

- The man-of-war's venom can be very painful to humans and, in very rare cases, it can kill if the victim has an allergic reaction to the sting.

- Loggerhead turtles eat Portuguese man-of-wars, along with sea jellies. The turtles' tough skin is too thick for the venom to penetrate.

It's hard to paddle the raft—the wind and the current make much more difference to where it's heading than you do with your paddle. But you manage to avoid the container, which is leaking a cargo of flip-flops into the sea. You're glad you decided to paddle, because you can see a jagged metal edge that could easily have spelled your doom.

Go to page 76.

You spread out your raft on the beach, holding it down with stones so that it dries out in the sun. Then you go off to search the forest edge for a good spot to make a shelter.

You find a bent tree that looks like a perfect spot. You drag some fallen logs out of the forest, first using a stick to check the forest floor for creepy-crawlies. Then you prop the logs up against the bent tree to make a lean-to shelter. You spread the raft material over it to make your shelter waterproof, and place more large rocks on it so that the material won't blow away. You find some broad leaves to go on the floor of the shelter, then spread your dry blankets out. You move all your other supplies into the shelter, feeling very pleased with your handiwork.

Go to page 98.

There's nothing wrong with eating insects, as long as you know what kind you're eating. Since there are poisonous kinds of almost every type of insect, you were foolish to eat the crickets without knowing for sure that they're an edible kind. But, luckily, the crickets you've caught and squished are not poisonous. You roast them over your fire, and they provide a tasty and nutritious source of protein.

But you can't live on crickets alone if you're going to survive on this island for awhile. You need fruit and vegetables, too, otherwise you might end up with scurvy—a horrible disease that's caused by lack of vitamin C. You spot a likely looking plant—its dried seed pods are filled with tasty looking bright red-and-black seeds.

If you decide to eat the plant, go to page 62.

If you decide not to, go to page 72.

Eating Insects

- Lots of people around the world eat insects as part of their daily diet. They have been doing it for thousands of years. Insect eating is practiced in Central and South America, Africa, and Asia.

- Some of the more popular insects eaten are crickets, grasshoppers, and ants, as well as scorpions and tarantulas (which are both arachnids, not insects). Sometimes it's the larval stage of the insect that is eaten.

- Eating insects is an ecological way to get your protein. For example, where people eat insects, no fields need to be cleared to graze cattle.

- Insects and arachnids are types of arthropods. Shellfish are in the same family group. People in Europe and North America don't like to even think about eating land-dwelling arthropods, but don't mind eating arthropods that live in the sea.

The raft floats toward the container, which is huge up close and is spilling out thousands of pairs of flip-flops into the sea. As you get closer, you realize the container has rusty, jagged metal edges. You try to paddle away from it, but it's too late. You're too close, and a gust of wind blows the raft up against the container and tears your raft.

The raft sinks quickly. You hang on to the container, but you don't last long.

The end.

Pacific Plastic

- Garbage in the sea, especially plastic, causes damage to sea life, ensnaring fish and marine mammals, and killing turtles who eat floating plastic bags, mistaking them for sea jellies.

- Because of the way the ocean's currents move, a lot of the garbage from all over the world ends up in the Great Pacific Garbage Patch—a large floating debris field in the ocean—mostly in the form of tiny pieces of plastic.

- There's an eastern and western section of the Garbage Patch. The eastern patch floats between Hawaii and the United States, and the western patch floats between Hawaii and Japan. They're connected by a current more than 5,600 miles (9,000 km) long, where the garbage floats.

- 90% of the garbage patch is plastic.

You run downhill as fast as you can, leaping over fallen logs and rocks, pushing aside creepers, your heart pounding. You have to get down to the beach and signal to the ship!

You fall, scratching yourself on a thorny plant, but get yourself up and dust yourself off before plunging onward to the beach. When you finally get there, you're completely out of breath. Panting, you put your hands on your knees and scan the sea for the ship.

It's there—but quite a long way away now. Is it worth sending up a distress flare?

If you decide to send a flare, go to page 73.

If you decide not to and wait for another ship, go to page 47.

You're eating breakfast one morning—bananas again—when something makes you look up. You're not sure, but you think you can see a ship—although it's very far away. Unless it's your mind playing tricks . . .

An hour later, you can tell it's definitely a ship! You try not to get too excited—maybe the ship won't come any closer. Even if it does, maybe it won't see your distress flares. You get the flares out of your shelter and read the instructions so you'll be ready when the ship is within range.

The ship still seems to be heading your way, but it looks as though it's starting to change course. You think it's close enough to spot your flare, but you're not sure. You decide to send a flare anyway. You fire it high into the sky in the direction of the ship.

You stare at the ship, willing it to change direction . . .

Go to page 114.

There don't seem to be any people living on the island, but you haven't explored it yet. There could be a village on the other side, for all you know. Some uninhabited islands in the South Pacific have vacation homes for tourists who want to experience life on a desert island. Even if there aren't any signs of life, you decide it would be silly not to explore it.

The island rises steeply in the middle—it's probably an ancient volcano. From the top of the thickly forested hill, you'll get a good view of the whole island. You set off, taking a bottle of water with you.

Go to page 52.

Volcanic Islands

- A volcano arises from a split in Earth's crust where hot molten magma from deep inside Earth erupts. Volcanic islands are formed when undersea volcanoes erupt over a long period of time, growing in size until they break the surface of the sea to form an island.

- The Hawaiian Islands are a chain of volcanic islands caused by a hot spot under one of the tectonic plates that forms Earth's crust. As this plate moves over the sea bed over millions of years, it moves the old volcano with it, and a new volcanic island is created over the hot spot. In Hawaii, the oldest island is a volcano millions of years old that is no longer active. In the distant future, new volcanic islands will probably form in the chain.

- The Galapagos Islands were also formed in this way, and so were the islands of Japan. In 2013, a new volcanic island popped up in the Pacific off the coast of Japan.

- Volcanic islands are also known as high islands. There are lots of volcanic islands in the South Pacific, some with volcanoes that are still active.

Yt;ou might be here for awhile. The shelter looks good, and your water needs are taken care of, whether you find a source of fresh water or not, because you have a desalinator. That just leaves food.

You start to have a look around and notice some rock pools on one side of the beach. Inside are some cone-shaped shells a bit longer than your hand. They look as though they might have creatures inside them that might be good to eat. Should you pick one up and find out? It would certainly be a very easy meal.

If you decide to try one of the animals, go to page 50.

If you decide not to try one and make a fire instead, go to page 40.

You wait until the ship is at its closest point, then stand at the open flap of your raft waving your T-shirt in the air wildly. You honk your horn, blow your whistle, and scream for all you're worth. You can't see anyone on board, but you keep making noise and waving anyway. The ship is surprisingly noisy as it churns past you. It shows no sign of slowing down.

Now you wonder whether it would have been better to risk sending a flare. (Actually, it wouldn't have—there's no one on lookout on the ship to see you or a flare anyway.) You watch the ship sail off into the distance toward land, hot food, and soft beds. You can't help imagining how different it must be on the ship instead of in this tiny raft. You feel more helpless and alone than ever.

Go to page 113.

By now, you've gotten used to fishing and collecting fruit to survive. You've spent time making improvements to your shelter. It's now more like a treehouse on stilts to keep you away from the ants, spiders, and other creepy-crawlies that sometimes crawl out of the forest. You don't often go into the forest and, every time you do, you make a careful search of the horizon for ships. You use rocks to spell out SOS in enormous letters on the beach, in case of a passing plane or helicopter.

After a few weeks, you see another ship. You don't have any flares left, but you make a smoky fire and jump up and down on the beach shouting and waving. The ship doesn't see you.

You survive for several months on the island. Thankfully, in the end, you're rescued even without a distress flare. A small plane spots your SOS and sends a rescue helicopter. Soon, you're looking forward to seeing your family and friends again. You are overjoyed when the pilot tells you that your uncle was found by fishermen only a day after the storm that washed him overboard.

The end.

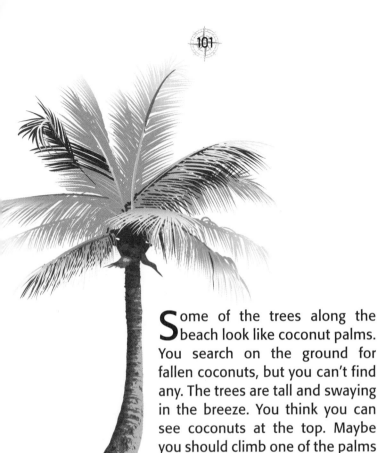

Some of the trees along the beach look like coconut palms. You search on the ground for fallen coconuts, but you can't find any. The trees are tall and swaying in the breeze. You think you can see coconuts at the top. Maybe you should climb one of the palms and gather some.

If you decide to climb a palm tree, go to page 82.

If you decide to look for fruit somewhere else, go to page 112.

You'll need to find plants to eat somewhere. You know that if you don't eat fresh fruit or vegetables, or find some other source of vitamin C, you'll get scurvy—a horrible disease that makes your gums bleed, your teeth drop out, and eventually kills you. You shudder at the idea.

You've spotted some seaweed—maybe you could eat that? Or maybe you should explore a bit further and see if you can find an edible plant somewhere else.

If you decide to eat some seaweed, go to page 106.

If you decide to look for something else, go to page 64.

The climb becomes steeper, and you're puffing and panting as you reach the top. You climb up on to bare rock above the tree line. There's a crater in the middle of the island. This must once have been a volcano, but it doesn't look as though it has erupted recently. You turn and look out across the island.

Your island is a circle of green in a turquoise sea. You can see the silver sand beach and cove where you've made your shelter. Rocks surround the rest of the island, which is covered in dense forest. It's beautiful, but there is no sign of humans.

Close to the island the water is light blue, becoming darker as the water deepens. As you scan the sea farther from the island, you spot something that makes your heart pound—it's a ship! You have to get back to the beach before it passes by!

Go to page 94.

You look out across the calm sea as your raft bobs along. The sun has come out, and the water is deep blue.

You spot something in the distance. You can't figure out what on Earth it might be. It looks like a sea of blue plastic, and you're heading straight for it. Soon you're in the midst of dozens of weird-looking transparent floating bags. Underneath them, long fronds reach down into the water.

Should you hook one with your paddle, and take a closer look? Maybe it's edible. On the other hand, perhaps these strange things are dangerous.

If you decide to take a closer look, go to page 86.

If you decide to leave them alone, go to page 110.

You continue uphill toward the middle of the island. You still feel as though someone—or something—is watching you, and you're seriously spooked for a while. But nothing happens. Maybe it was some kind of harmless animal.

Go to page 103.

You gather some of the seaweed. It doesn't look that appetizing, but it's an easy way of getting your greens. You've heard that seaweed is a common food in the South Pacific, and you can see why—there's lots of it.

You clean the seaweed and try a bit raw. It tastes OK, but you decide to boil it up in some water over your fire instead. You might like it a bit better that way.

Although seaweed is indeed eaten in the South Pacific, you were unwise to eat some without knowing for sure that it's an edible kind. Some types of seaweed can upset your stomach, which is the last thing you need in a survival situation.

It might be good to find some fish to go with your seaweed.

Go to page 83.

Edible Seaweeds

- Seaweeds are an important part of the South Pacific diet. They are eaten in Fiji and other South Pacific islands.

- Several different kinds of seaweeds are collected from shallow lagoons and reefs, mainly by women and girls. The seaweeds are harvested from different areas in a cycle lasting a few weeks, so that they can grow back ready for the next harvest.

- Different types of seaweeds are eaten in different ways. Some are cooked and some eaten raw, with different flavorings, including lemon juice and chili.

- Seaweeds are eaten in many other parts of the world, too. Laver is a type of seaweed eaten in China, Japan, and Korea. More and more seaweeds are being eating in North America now, too.

You look up, and almost scream from fright. About 25 pairs of eyes are staring at you from a tree a short distance away!

They are huge, furry bats hanging upside down from the branches, with their leathery wings wrapped around them. Most of them are asleep, but some have opened their eyes and are staring at you with interest. Now that you're over the initial shock, they look kind of cute, with beautiful big brown eyes. You don't go any nearer—you don't want to alarm them. But you watch them for a bit before you head back uphill, toward the middle of the island, leaving the bats to go back to sleep.

Go to page 103.

Fruit Bats

- Fruit bats are also known as flying foxes or megabats, and are some of the world's largest bats. There are lots of different kinds—the largest have a wingspan of up to 5.5 feet (1.7 m). The smallest kind is only two inches (6 cm) long.

- On some South Pacific islands, fruit bats (and sometimes other smaller bat species) are the only native land mammals.

- As the name suggests, fruit bats eat fruit, and some eat nectar from flowers. On some Pacific islands, they're seen as a pest and are hunted.

- These large bats don't use echolocation like other bats do. Instead they use a highly developed sense of smell, and large eyes that are adapted to seeing in twilight and dark forests. There's one exception: the Egyptian fruit bat uses echolocation.

- Fruit bats are sometimes hunted for food in the South Pacific—apparently they taste delicious.

- Fruit bats have been known to carry viruses that are fatal to humans, though the bats don't get sick themselves. So it's just as well you didn't get too close.

You watch the floating things warily for signs they might harm you or the raft in some way. But they just drift along in the current. They don't seem as though they're aware of you being there at all. These creatures are known as Portuguese man-of-wars (see page 87) and they sting, so it's a good thing you didn't touch one.

Soon the wind picks up and you lose sight of the strange animals. You sleep on and off for the rest of the day and into the night. You wake up and look out of your raft. The sky is studded with stars, and you open the canopy, lay back, and watch them for a while . . . when suddenly you hear what sounds like surf breaking on a beach! You jump up and look out—there's an island not far away! You start to paddle as fast as you can toward the beach.

Go to page 70.

You drink some water from the bottle in the Grab Bag. But you don't feel any better–if anything you feel worse. Soon, you feel dizzy and confused, so you lie down.

Low levels of salt in your body have led to hyponatremia (see page 57). Your body is unable to process water without salt, and the cells in your body are expanding. You're feeling dizzy because the cells in your brain are expanding.

You fall into a coma and die.

The end.

It's not long before you find a fruit you definitely recognize—bananas. Some of the fruit is yellow and ripe, and you eat it hungrily. It tastes delicious.

Bananas contain vitamin C, although they aren't as good a source as oranges and other types of citrus fruit. But you should get enough of it to ward off scurvy.

Go to page 96.

You feel awful. And it's not just because of the rapidly disappearing ship. You have a pounding headache, and you feel weak and tired. You wonder if it might be a good idea to drink some more water. Or maybe you should find some salt to eat. You know that a low level of salt in the body is just as dangerous as not drinking enough water, especially when you've been sweating.

If you decide to drink some water, go to page 111.

If you decide to eat salt, go to page 56.

Your heart is pounding as you wait desperately for the ship to turn—and it does!

It's a cruise ship, full of happy vacationers. It makes an unscheduled stop close to your island. By this time, you're jumping up and down, waving, and crying with relief. Some of the crew get into a dinghy and motor across the shallower water to your beach. You ask the crew about your uncle and discover some good news—he was found by fishermen only a day after the storm that washed him overboard! Relieved, you're soon looking forward to a hot meal, a comfortable bed, and seeing your family and friends again.

You're safe at last!

The end.

People of the South Pacific

People crossed thousands of miles of open sea from continent to continent to discover the remote South Pacific islands. They came by canoe, navigating by the stars, 1,700 years before European or Chinese explorers managed to make long sea voyages. They settled on islands scattered across nearly 12,000 square miles (30,000 square km) of the Pacific Ocean. Different cultures grew up on the different island groups.

People first colonized the Pacific islands around 50,000 years ago, arriving in New Guinea from Asia and the Indonesian islands. The first South Pacific long-distance seafarers were known as the Lapita. They traveled from New Guinea to colonize islands farther east more than 3,000 years ago. With nothing more to help them navigate than the stars, they managed to bring people, animals, farming equipment, and plants across the vast Pacific. They colonized the Solomon Islands first, then moved on to the Santa Cruz Islands 250 miles (400 km) to the east. Across another 500 miles (800 km) of empty ocean, Fiji was colonized next. Eventually, between 300 and 900 CE, people spread all the way to Hawaii, the Cook Islands, Easter Island, and New Zealand.

The Pacific islands were colonized by Europeans, like most of the rest of the world, starting in the 1500s. Today, most islands are independent. A few still belong to the United States, France, Chile, and New Zealand.

Real-life Lost-at-Sea Stories
Adrift in a Life Raft

Poon Lim holds the record for lost-at-sea survival. He survived 133 days on a lifeboat in the South Pacific in 1942–43, after the British merchant ship he worked on was torpedoed and sunk during World War II. He survived for a couple of hours in the sea wearing a life jacket, then boarded a life boat he found drifting. There were some supplies in the boat. Poon Lim also caught fish (including a small shark) and seabirds, and collected rainwater. He was finally rescued close to land by some Brazilian fishermen.

William and Simone Butler survived 66 days adrift in a small life raft in the Pacific Ocean in June 1989. Their yacht had been attacked by a group of pilot whales and it sank. They drifted hundreds of miles toward the coast of Costa Rica, where they were eventually rescued. They survived by catching and eating fish and turtles. They also had a desalinator, without which they might not have survived.

Steven Callahan was sailing his yacht solo across the Atlantic Ocean in 1982, when it collided with a whale and sank. He abandoned ship and took to his life raft. He was rescued by fishermen within sight of land 76 days later. He had almost four quarts (4 L) of water and two solar stills and, like the Butlers and Poon Lim, he survived on fish and seabirds. Also like them, Callaghan spotted various ships on the open sea, none of which saw him.

Paul Lucas didn't even have a life raft! In 2000, he was diving off the coast of Australia when he drifted too far out in stormy seas. He spent 24 hours floating in his wetsuit, then spotted an island and swam to it. He was rescued soon afterward.

Desert Island Survivors

In 1722, **Philip Ashton** was captured by pirates. When they stopped at the uninhabited island of Roatan, off the coast of Honduras, Ashton escaped and hid in the jungle until the pirates left. He survived on the island for over a year before he was rescued in 1724.

It was **Tom Neale's** dream to live on a desert island. In 1952, he was left on Suwarrow atoll in the Cook Islands, where he lived happily all alone. He left the island because of illness, but returned from 1960 to 1963, and again for a final ten-year stay from 1967 to 1977 before he died.

Galapagos Islands

Located 575 miles (926 km) west of Ecuador, the Galapagos Islands are a chain of volcanic islands that straddle the Equator. Because the islands are volcanic, and as such, have never been connected to a continent, every species that lives here originally arrived here either by flying, swimming, or floating! The largest animal on the islands is the giant Galapagos tortoise. There are no natural predators on the islands.

As a young man, naturalist Charles Darwin first traveled to the Galapagos Islands on board the HMS *Beagle*, a ship that had been dispatched to find harbors as Britain expanded its empire. While in the Galapagos, Darwin noticed that while the animals and plants were similar from island to island, they had adaptations that helped them fit perfectly with their environments. Along with other research, Darwin's time in the Galapagos Islands eventually led to him writing *The Origin of Species*, the first book to ever explain how plants and animals have evolved over time to suit their environments.

Drinking Seawater: A Death Sentence

Your body needs both salt and water to survive. But if there's too much of one and not enough of the other, bad things can happen.

While your body is equipped to process small amounts of salt, sea water has far more salt than you can safely ingest—about four times as much. The body dilutes incoming salt with liquids to keep the salt at a safe level. That's why you're always thirsty half an hour after eating bacon or a grilled-cheese sandwich.

If you take in too much salt, your body will take water from every cell in order to try and dilute it before excreting it as urine. This process shrinks your cells, leading to muscle cramps and constriction of your blood vessels. Blood flow to your brain slows, and you become dizzy and disoriented. Eventually, the excess salt dehydrates your body, leading to organ failure and death.

Glossary

barnacles Shellfish that attach themselves to rocks or other underwater surfaces

bilge pump Pump that removes water from the bottom of a boat

buoyant Able to float

canister Cylinder-shaped container

colonized Land taken control of by people from another country

condenses Changes into liquid

contaminated Unclean

dehydrated Suffering from a lack of water

dorsal Toward the back

echolocation Using the echoes of calls to figure out how far away objects are

embers Hot, glowing coals that remain after a fire goes out

harpoon Long, spear-like instrument

hyponatremia Lack of salt in the blood

hypothermia Dangerously low body temperature

kindling Small, dry twigs that will burn quickly and easily; used for lighting a fire

lagoon Shallow body of water separated by islands or reefs from a larger body of water

listing Leaning

parasite A creature that lives by attaching itself to and feeding on another creature

phosphorescence Light generated by marine animals and plants

pod Group of dolphins

regurgitate Bring swallowed food out of the mouth

scurvy Deadly disease caused by a lack of vitamin C

sterile Free from germs

submerged Under water

tinder Very dry material that is easy to set on fire

torpedo Weapon propelled under water toward a target

toxin Poisonous substance

venomous Capable of injecting venom (poison)

Learning More

Bailey, Gerry. *Stranded on an Island: Can Science Save Your Life?* (Science to the Rescue) Crabtree Publishing, 2014.

Callahan, Steven. *Adrift: Seventy-six Days Lost at Sea.* Mariner Books, 2002.

Defoe, Daniel. *Robinson Crusoe.* William Collins, 2010.

Jackson, Tom. *Shark Attack.* (Crabtree Contact) Crabtree Publishing, 2008.

Johnson, Robin. *Titanic.* (Crabtree Chrome) Crabtree Publishing, 2013.

Korman, Gordon. *Island—Book One: Shipwreck.* Scholastic, 2001.

Korman, Gordon. *Island—Book Two: Survival.* Scholastic, 2001.

Korman, Gordon. *Island—Book Three: Escape.* Scholastic, 2001.

Tarshis, Lauren. I Survived series. Scholastic, 2010–2014

Websites

Survival at Sea
http://www.survival-expert.com/Adrift_at_Sea.htm

Making a Solar Still
www.youtube.com/watch?v=PP9D0M2nS0A

How to survive on a desert island (The Telegraph)
www.telegraph.co.uk/travel/travelnews/travel-
truths/10610251/How-to-survive-on-a-desert-island.html

Survival Guide on a Deserted Island (USA Today)
http://traveltips.usatoday.com/survival-guide-deserted-
island-62359.html

Types of Shelter
www.wilderness-survival.net/shelters-2.php

**Pacific island travel with author David Stanley (The South
Pacific Organizer)**
www.southpacific.org/index.html

Index